JESTFUL GESTS:

EVERYTHING UNDER THE SUN

TARIQ ISMAIL

*To humans, who are now overly familiar with the words pandemic,
lockdown, quarantine, virus and "I'm sorry, we did everything we
could". Despite the hardships and the losses, somehow, miraculously,
we're still moving and enjoying the sunshine.*

"Young cat! If you keep
your eyes open enough,
oh, the stuff you will learn!
The most wonderful stuff!"

- Dr Seuss, *I Can Read With My Eyes Shut!*

Here comes the kitten, smaller than a shoe
Here comes her color and her story too
Her coat shines orange like sunset and fire
So shines her story, something to admire

I

FISHCAKES

EVERYTHING UNDER THE SUN

Here comes the kitten, smaller than a shoe
Here is her color, burnt and ragged
How strong this baby is to move forward
On these dry streets that hold no water

She is comprised of the tiniest bits:
Of the tiniest nose and the tiniest ears
And the tiniest eyes, so tiny in their wonder
Even the ticks that suckle her are tinier than tiny

Her power is not tiny. Never that.
Not her curiosity. Never that.
Not her endurance. Never that.
The paradoxical mighty in the tiniest of tiny.

A whole entire world exists on this tiny street:
Here be the birthplace where she first opened her eyes
Here be the shelter where she had her first dream
Here be the graveyard where her mother fell deep into sleep

Here in this place where all was undone
Where all could be found, everything under the sun

Such a fateful day arrives when the kitten looms large
Dozing outside the graveyard, watching the people go past
There one bends to look at her, different from the rest
Is tiny like her, with a tiny face and big tiny eyes

The tiny hands curl over the tiny orange body
Tiny little fingers stroking the tiny shafts of orange fur
The combined heat of her orange and his palms
Injects marrow into this hollowed-out kitten

Such a dream it is, and yet it is not,
To be lifted from the everything street
That is all at once a birthplace and a shelter and a graveyard
And placed into the heart of this tiny person

A tiny spark flares in this anarchic place of undone
Where all could be found, everything under the sun
But not everything, no, this place is *not* a microcosmic dome
For it is everything except a home

SHOEBOX

His name is Boy
And her name is Kitty

It is the strangest of things for her
To be looked at from this angle
Of want and desire

So used to being kicked over the terrace
And having the flying remnants of boney tuna
Flung into her face

Such a tiny creature with sprinklings of dirt
Discoloring her fiery amberish coat
Choked by the neck until her lungs collapse

Boy picks her up far too often, but she does not mind
How relieving it is to feel the warmth compress of a gentle hand
And not the strike of a heated malicious fist

How tasteful to be lifted up and not flung
Off the rugged path and not onto it
Pressed against the musical vibrations of Boy's heart

She vibrates along with the rhythm of his love
Stares up at him with the most curious eyes
The pools of pupils expanding to oceans of tangible shadow

So too do his eyes expand, wish-washing with tears
That plop onto her battered, scarred whiskers
It drips into her mouth, hydrates her chapped yellow tongue

There come a point, an irreversible, absolute, fatal point
Where he does not put her back down onto the deranged road
But tucks her tiny bottom into his palm and encloses her in his jacket

Aeons later, he places her tiny body into a shoebox
She peeps over the lid, sees his lips tinker:
"I'm taking you home."

She snuggles into that chasmic shoebox
And he feeds her a fishcake, so tender and fishy and hot
Bits of it crumble over the shoebox and land on his lap

II

MILK

ON THE COMPLEXITY OF A CAT POST

Can you call me by my name?
Which one, we say? There are many.
Kitty, says Boy and Girl
Ma says I should look up to Girl
"Such a woman will guide you toward the right
And show you how to maneuver this unsteerable world
Respect the old magic running through her blood
By calling her *didi*."
Neenee, says Papa, for the one who possesses
The gift of persuasion
CC, says Ma, for the child who conquers
Through cheerful curiosity

I look at these chattering fools
And then back
At the seven-foot monstrosity
Of pillars and fluffy foam pads
Such a thing needs no prelude or introduction
All I must trust in is that it is powerful enough
And will endure
My weight and nails
I shake my bottom and arch my back and see,
In the reflection of the stained window
These people, who argue over my name,
Watching as I pounce onto the cat post
I claw my way to the top
Pulling loose a few strings
On the way up

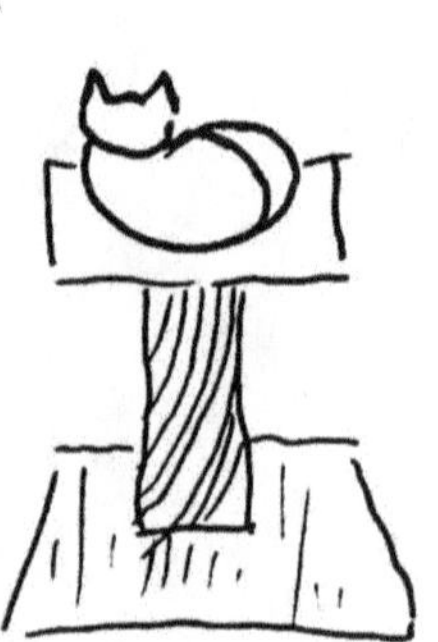

WISE OBSERVATIONS ABOUT EARTHLY ENDEAVOURS

Is there anything more divine
Than a glass of iced milk?

Perhaps it is the boop of my head
As I bump against the pads of Boy's toes

Perhaps it is the scraping of my pink tongue
As it cleans Papa's greasy curry-laced fingers

Perhaps it is the weighted breathlessness in my lungs
Brought on by Girl chasing me around the cat post

Perhaps it is the tingle and rush of comfort
From when Ma gently combs my fur into place

Perhaps it is the hug of the crackling crispy firewood
Toasting our snuggling bodies on a bitter winter's evening

Perhaps it is my tiny body surfing up and down on Boy
As he snores loudly into the night, drowning out my purring

Perhaps it is the yearning in my paws as I run toward them

Each of them extending out their arms and yelling my names

"Kitty! Neenee! CC!"

Each of them lavishly competing for my love

Perhaps it is all of these things…?

Nay, it is none of these things!

Because even my tiny existence in this place has taught me

That there is nothing more divine than a glass of iced milk

III

LICORICE

LICORICE FUR

Let this crispy white page

Be evidence of my despair

Let it be the blank canvas

Where I may write my obituary

Today is a day of betrayals

Where my loving, thoughtful pride

Of babbling blissful boneheads

Have sucked the beat out of my heart

They've imposed a nuisance on me

Something as invasive as the taste of licorice

Today, this day of betrayals, is such a day

For they have brought into my home, my space…

Another cat

WOE AND DESPAIR! Wail alongside my corpse!
Mourn with me over spilled, wasted milk!
They've let the thing loose to wander around
Such a monstrous, hideous, tiny thing

Its eyes are like butter, its candy nose
As pink as the lily petals in the garden
It smells like baked flour, so sickly sweet
Its fur is licorice, bug-black and sticky

...

They've locked me away!
Only because I ran up to the vile creature
And gave it a smack! Gave it a boop! No, not a boop,
A bop! A hard, vicious bop!

Ma has disappointedly sat my solemn face down
"Have these cushioned walls made you forget already?
The ancient blood running in us? We have taught *you*.
And now you will teach *her*. You are now her *didi*."

I approach the scrawny creature, suspiciously sniffing
She awakens from her lullabies, looks at me with no judgement
She stretches up with all her might
And plants a kiss on my cheek

Such a tender thing, this kiss, so innocent and warm
So much like Boy's beating heart and Girl's head massages
I glare at the thing then plop beside it to warm its bones
Not because I suddenly care but because Ma said I should

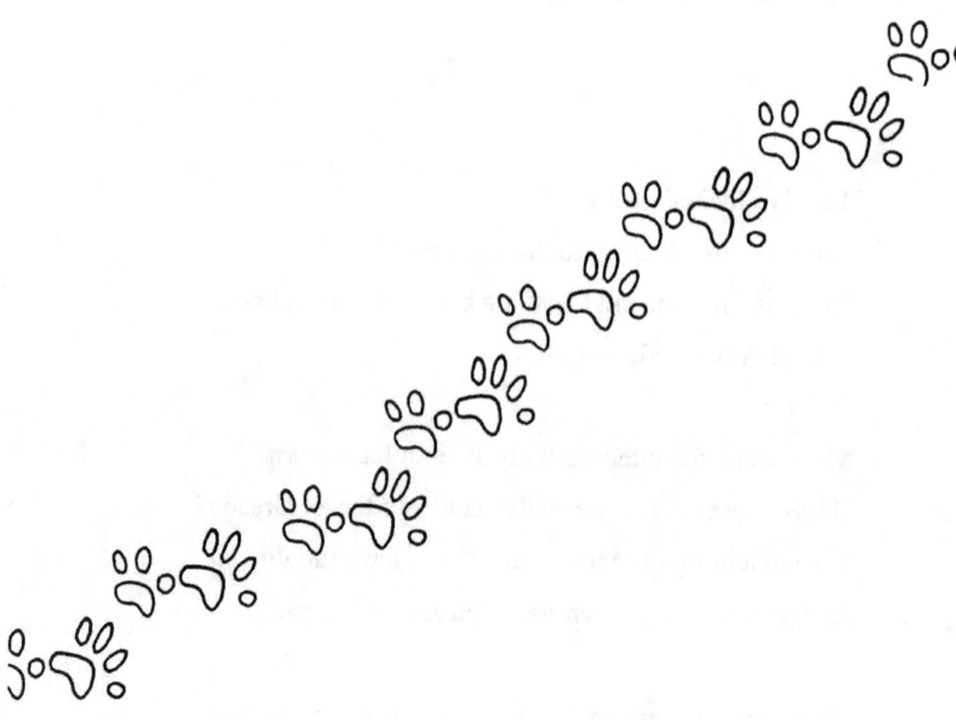

THE MOST IMPORTANT TOOL IN SIBLINGHOOD

The most important tool to have

In this vast and chaotic battlefield

Is not the grandest of swords

Or the bulkiest of shields

Neither is it the rawness of magic

Or the resilience of wisdom

No.

The mightiest tool to hold

Against the terror that is siblinghood

Is a measuring scale

So that when milk is poured

Or when the fishy food is served

The scale provides hard empirical evidence

And absolute certainty

That they do not have more than you

TOM CAT

A *didi* is an artist in their highest form
A writer, a poet, a magician with letters
Able to collect words into a bucket
And form elaborate illusions

Baby – that's what we call her – requires this skill from me
Demands I be able to convince Ma of stories
That do not exist
And I do, even though I threaten I won't every day

She sneaks off into the starlit night
With a manly bugger named Tom
Who is the Prince of some unheard-of litter across the field
They hold priceless jewels he has promised to Baby

I've only ever seen his silhouette in the shadows
Wonder if their love is real or even attainable
I blast her with questions about her escapades of the night
Only for her to lustfully sigh and curl up in a ball

Baby forgets about the dirt in her nails
Ma demands if there was a window left open
She fritters and looks at me pleadingly
So I save her. Again. Of course I do.

Such mistakes, flaws made repeatedly
But I know she'll keep making them
Because how else will she experience experiences
And remain interested in life?

She makes the mistake that night (like all nights before)
Accompanied by my incessant complaining. But as she slips out
To the tall bulking shadow, even I cannot deny
That the freeing air pulsates with an electrifying hunger

IV

FLORA

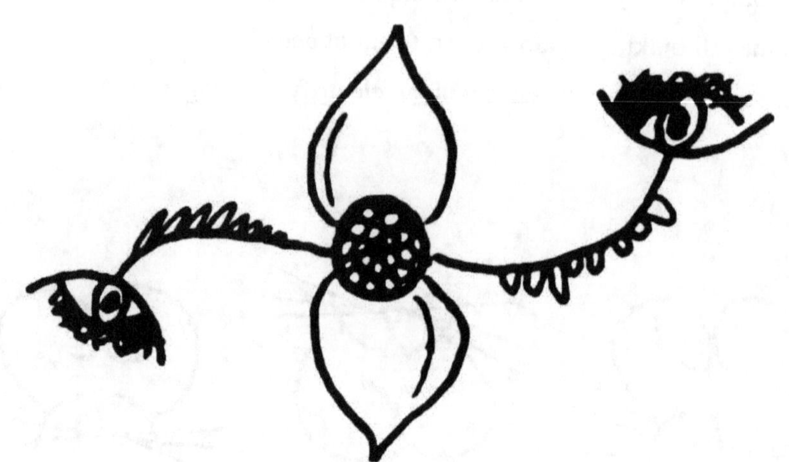

CAT EYE

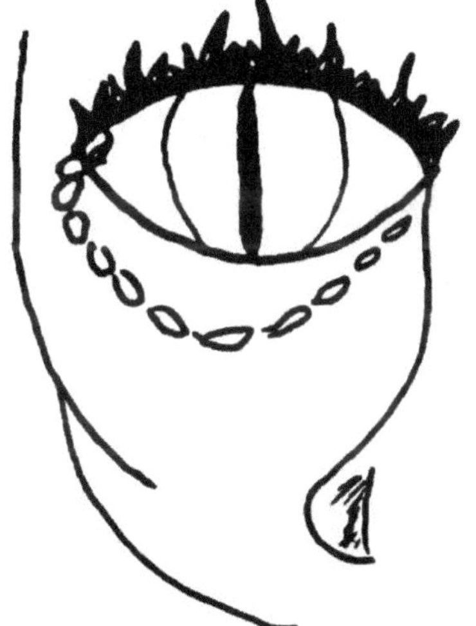

How odd to imagine a time
Where the earth around me wasn't rich
And black and colorful and pleasing
What a privilege to begin the day
Outside in this great beyond
Nestling my orange coat
Against the prickly grass blades
How I look forward to liquifying myself
In the pocket of shade underneath the tree
And to stare at the petite honeybees
This is the place where I am hydrated
Where my mind knows only sanctity
Migration moves with the sky's transition
From baby yellow to violent purple
What great effort it takes to go away
But not before I make a stop at the glassy pool
Where, as I lap up the water, I see the reflection
Of a cat eye

BOOP BOP BOOP

Amongst the thinning branches of the rose bush
I perch myself up lazily against the anthill
Gazing upon the sunny day objectively

From the corner of my eye I see her licorice bum
Shaking left to right, left to right in the floating grass
A FLASH! and then she's on top of me
Toppling me into the freshly tilled soil
Where the earthworms are building their home

I yowl at her and we chase each other around
This very lush floral garden
That only knows the peace of songbirds

Baby's licorice bum is plumpy but swift
She swerves around and mockingly boops my head
When I catch her
I don't just boop her
But bop her hard on the knob

BOP BOP BOP BOP BOP
An appropriate punishment
For ruining a perfectly good morning

Suddenly the game is no longer a game

Has become something serious

Our nails utilized as intended by evolution

Ma has to come outside to separate us

From clawing each other's eyes out

WATER

Baby and I perch on the sea blue counters
        The coldness of the marble sweeping over us
                Like the music from the speaker washing over Ma
        As she throws the pans into bubbling soapy water
And swipes the sweat pimpling on her brow
        The tune playing is as immersive as a wave
                Going up and down and sucking you in
                        To our tiny peripheral cat ears
                                It is as loud as the roaring echo in a seashell
                                        "Listen to that!" Ma exclaims, skipping,
                                                "The Connection."
                Orange and licorice ears turn toward the cooling sound
                        Heads swaying like water molecules in wind
        "Connecting all of us is not this shared earth
        But the swaying of water
The One being that flows through all of us
        That has power over all things."
                We all dance in the intimate space
                        Feeling the rhythm of water within
                                Understanding movement and not language
                                        Letting the swish of the water music
                        Drown out the looming scent from the stove
        The odor of burning oil

V

KIBBLE

GREY SCALE

Happens so quickly.
The world moves
From a place
Of tranquil perfection
To something devoid
Of all color
And juvenile ignorance.
Grey scale world.
There is nothing
In this desert.
Only the crunching
Of dried kibble.

TELLER TATTLER TALER

Chittering chatter breaks out

Amongst the square brown boxes

The Teller who is a dog

A fluffy brown Pekingese

Says he is sure they are taking us

To some forbidden place

Where teeth will be weaved into chains

And paws will be made into gloves

The crowd goes wild with fear.

Scampering scatters reverberate around the cages

Tools of restraint effective to imprison

The Tattler who is a bird

A rainbow macaw

Says she is sure they are taking us

To some heavenly place

Overflowing with delicious delights and gardens

The crowd goes wild with want.

Tittering twitters spear the darkness

Cutting through this dank place that smells of farm hay

The Taler who is cat

A wise and remarkably unbroken Nebelung

Whispers into the blackness

That these tales of misfortune and jewels

Are nothing but that

Tales

That the journey is going to be much more

Flat

The crowd silences itself...

Then they boo the Nebelung

And start to debate about who will go

To the doom of the teller

Or the haven of the tattler

Forgetting entirely

About the taler and his uninteresting imagination

VI

HALF & HALF

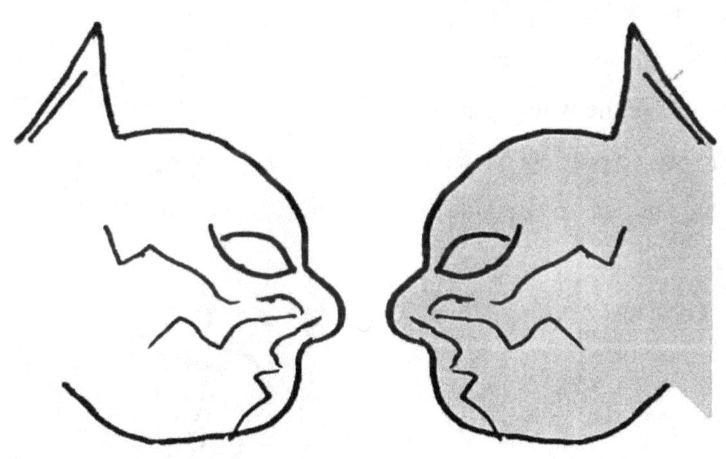

WHERE THE WOOD CREAKS

In this ugly ancient house
I cannot live fully
Fun becomes stagnant and laden with algae
Because the floors are hypocrites
Who give away our stealthy locations
I look for the nooks and crannies
But each spot is illuminated
By the shrieking of the wood

How I miss the solitude
Of having soundproof floors
That silence the vibrations
That wiggle off the vinyl
Here where the wood is authentic
There are no pockets of shadow
Worthy enough to contain spilled secrets
Such privilege
To have silent synthetic floors

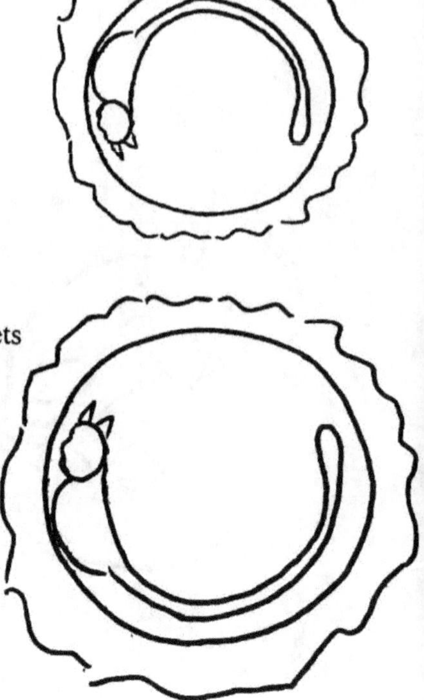

BRITTLE EARTH

Such cracked dusty earth in this place
So uneventful and dry
Wholly unfeeling
And without personality

Where is the lush vegetation
Coated in crystallized frost?
Where are those suckling honeybees
And their dustings of fairy pollen?

In this arid land
The bees are as big as Baby's eyes
They don't twitter around with a bzzzz
But skyrocket through the windows with a SCREECH!

How depressing to think the happiest memories
Can induce so much sad longing
I see the tears in Ma's eyes
Salty enough to nourish this barren land

SPLIT MILK

I lap up the cold white fluid
Spit it out onto the floor in confusion
Too thick to be milk
Too thin to be cream
It curdles on the floor
And becomes cheese

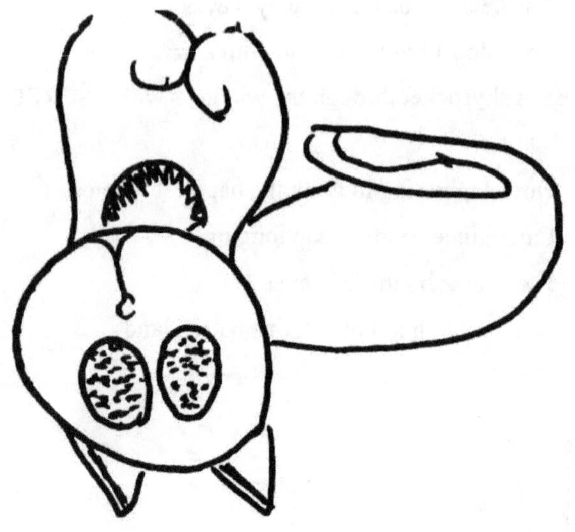

VII

BIRD BONE

GENESIS

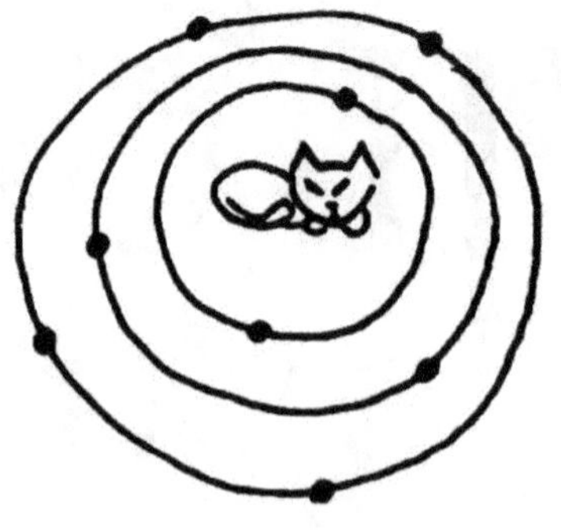

I'm perched on the kitchen counter
Distanced from an isolated Ma
Who is concentrating on frying vetkoek
She tosses them around over and over
Until they puff up into perfect spheres
Golden and airy and beautiful
They swirl around in orbits
Immersed in the golden solar flare of the bubbling oil
Boy and Girl burst their way in
Two hyperactive stars
Magnetized by the sizzling fat
Ma kisses them on their foreheads
And hands them fresh red apples to eat
Warns them to keep away from the vetkoek
When Ma leaves, Baby strolls in
A pathetically sly look on her face
She hops onto the counter smooth as a snake
Grabs a vetkoek with her gnashing jaws
Hops off and scampers away with the sphere in her mouth
Boy and Girl are inspired, moved
By the prowess of the cat's audacity
They too steal the vetkoek
Ma comes in and sees their greedy hands

Clawing at her handmade food

She storms after them and shoos them away

Cursing them to eternal damnation

Promising she hates them for their betrayal

But she doesn't

She loves them with her entire being

Because as soon as they leave

She returns to the stove

Making sure the spheres are more than edible

That they are perfect in their flavor and appearance too

I gaze at her with wonder

Wondering about her mysteries

It seems like such a lonely place to be right at the top

Mixing molecules without companionship

So far away from everything

And yet so close, so very close

Ready to catch you if you were to fall

My staring disrupts her routine

And she turns around to plant a kiss on my forehead

She sneaks a bit of raw dough from the bowl

And lets me clean it off her finger

When I'm done she opens the faucet

And lets me suckle at the water

She giggles at my clumsy drinking and smiles at me

Not as if I were a four-legged creature

But as if she birthed me.

FILTERED STARLIGHT

Ma closes the window net
To keep the mosquitos out
Even during the day
When there are no mosquitos present
Yearning for the outside is no help
So I sit right by the window to pretend
Let the sun filtering in
Absorb into the folds of my fur
Some days it works – the heat tricks me
Makes me believe I am outside amongst life
Other days not – on those days
My insides are as hollow
As the bones of the birds that mock me
From beyond the window's net

VIII

SCALLOPS

Yesterday Pappa told us:

"Go on kittens, hide away your toys!
Make sure you're quiet and don't make noise
Shut your doors tight and slip on your socks
So as not to awaken the fox
who lurks within these deceiving parts
And salivates for your little hearts!"

SWEATY DREAM

I had a dream that Baby the Innocent Cat
Had her tiny head go ka-splat!
Out in the garden she ran and hid
But she could not bid
That the fox would sniff her out
I dreamed that her licorice snout
Was grabbed by the fox and bitten
Needless to say that this kitten
Did not last very long, not at all
I panicked as her eyes became small
The fur changing to blood clouded my sight
I yowled and awoke with a fright
Perspiring and gleaning, gasping and weeping
Only to see her next to me sleeping

GINGER FOX

Pappa warned us the other day
To not go running outside
For there were whispers of the presence
Of a ginger fox
"This fox is dirty
Will pounce on you from behind."
No matter how much the oxygen calls to me
I yield away
Because the fresh image of the ginger fox
Leaks into my brain
I peek through the net, unable to cease my yearning
When I see a flash of licorice black from beyond my barrier
Shining ever so brightly in the heat of the day
I scamper to Baby's room
She's nowhere to be seen
Run back to the window and freeze in terror
See Baby do what Baby does best
She's rolling around dirtying her coat
Totally blissful, totally unaware
Behind her
The slow retreat of the forest branches
The flash of a ginger coat

FORTIFIED FALSIFIED FORTUNES

Clouds gather like solemn soldiers
All clad in black and brooding
Ma's tears are no longer singular
They shower the roughly made grave

Pappa clings onto a distraught Girl
Both cannot contain their grief
Joining Ma and her theatrics
Watering the disturbed earth

Boy stands like the clouds
Rigid
But full of water
Ready to burst

I watch from behind the window net
An unmoved specimen
Who has survived more than this
Pesky turn of events

I wander into the undisturbed kitchen
Hop atop the counter like Baby would have
Drawn in by the smell of whatever's on top
There's baked scallops in a tray, cold and untouched

I slide one into my mouth – immediately spit it out
I sneer at the wet scallop in disgust
Not the tasty morsel it looked like it was
Just a counterfeit fishcake

IX

BUTTER

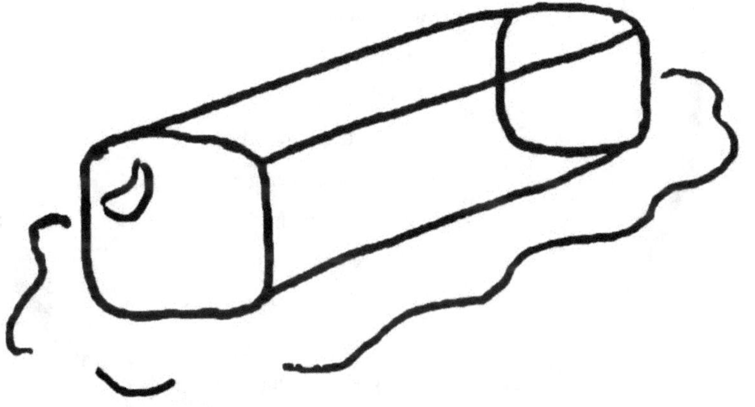

BORGE

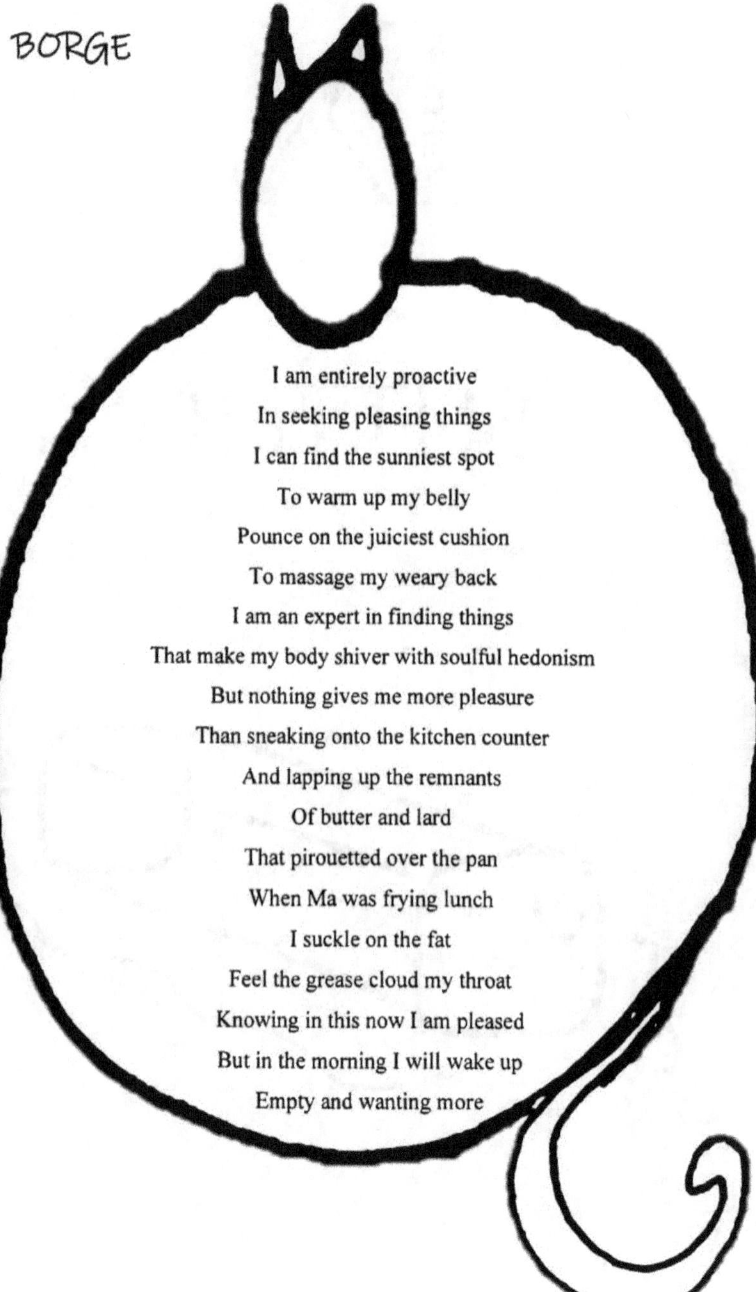

I am entirely proactive
In seeking pleasing things
I can find the sunniest spot
To warm up my belly
Pounce on the juiciest cushion
To massage my weary back
I am an expert in finding things
That make my body shiver with soulful hedonism
But nothing gives me more pleasure
Than sneaking onto the kitchen counter
And lapping up the remnants
Of butter and lard
That pirouetted over the pan
When Ma was frying lunch
I suckle on the fat
Feel the grease cloud my throat
Knowing in this now I am pleased
But in the morning I will wake up
Empty and wanting more

GLUTTONY MUTTONY

I've become a stealthy expert
At slithering on the granite counter
To find morsels of anything to ravish

I lap up the oil and the milk
Gorge on whole mouthfuls of lamb
So tender, so fatty

It becomes athletic
To eat with such fervor
Swallowing chunks without chewing

Plentiful temporary delights
All sweet, all greasy, too much *all*
There is no in between or equilibrium

I make the mistake, the grotesque mistake
Of eating in front of a mirror
That horrid sheet of truths

I see myself disheveled and fat and abundant
Mouth sopping wet with melted fat and chunks of a spud
Eyes tiny with greed, so animalistic and dehydrated

What a horrid, horrid error

To expose myself to this sheet of truths

I gorge on more greasy lamb to forget my error

X

SRIRACHA

WHAT?

Plumped up on my throne of cushions
Staring aimlessly at the garden
So devoid of anything
Save for the wound of the graveyard out front
Ma comes to where I lounge
Probably to be kind
I deny her that luxury
By shooting a sneer at her
Making sure she knows
I want to be left alone
In my pointless existence

LMA

Please don't come bother me
While I'm trying to exist
In this pathetic excuse of a sun

I don't like you
Or anything else

Leave me alone.

XI

EMPTY SILVER
BOWL

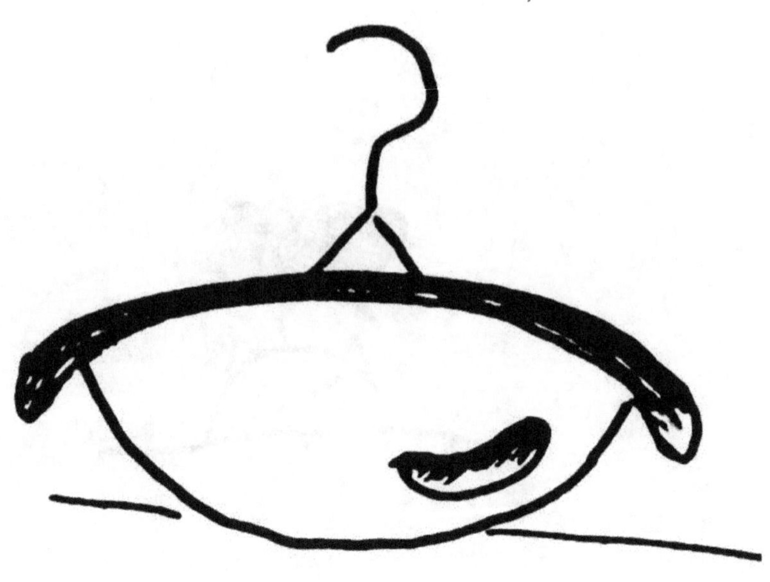

WHAT'S ON MY FACE?

A day arrives

When I sit by my empty silver bowl

Waiting for something to gorge on

As I am waiting

I peer down into the silver depths

To see a bland orange face staring back

As idle as the bowl

Robbed of life and color

Ma comes in with the kibble

And sees the bowl flooded with salty liquid

She looks at me quizzingly

I tell her I hate her

But not to take it personally

Because what I claim I feel for her

Is a millionth of what I feel for myself

I walk away from the wettened bowl

Which lies in front of the locked cupboard

Where the second bowl sits

Empty and unused

UNDERWATER

Sometimes I just want to go

Deep down down deep

Underneath the riptide

Fully immersed in the echoey silence

The want to lick

Salt mixed with saliva

Is more than the desire

To come up for air

I don't want to come up for oxygen

Or reflect on my sins and flaws

I just want to float down, down

And let music steer my sinking

XII

CHOCOLATE

BY THE STONEY GRAVEYARD

Gorging on food again, nothing new
This time it's chicken and potatoes
Roasted heavily in garlic and olive oil
One of the potatoes rolls off the counter
Onto the floor
Out the kitchen
Through the front door
Into the garden
Stops in front of the grave
I approach it hesitantly
Unsure of what to do
But greedy enough to still want the potato
Such a journey to get there
That when I arrive at the tombstone
I am breathless
And fat
Frozen in front of the dry packed sand
Such a barren inescapable wasteland
I stare at the lumps of rock embedded in the mound
Wandering what's hidden beneath it
Suddenly the breathlessness is replaced by something darker
My insides turn the other way around
A loud shattering smashes my eardrums

Not water music at all

But the screeching of those monstrous bees

So large, so loud, so lavish

Can't escape

My face is bleeding out liquid

Watering the cursed grave

Seeping beneath the surface

To hydrate whatever lies beneath

I bolt back inside, ginger clouding my vision

Jump back on the counter

Swallow a whole brick of butter

Not enough butter, not enough

I throw myself into the cupboard

Hide in the airy darkness

I see a bar of chocolate

Swallow one piece

Two pieces

Then the whole slab

Because it *is* enough

To poison my insides

And make my brain drunk

It helps me forget

That looming feeling of hurt

That black feeling of death

Washes away that invasive flavor

Of licorice on my tongue

SWEET TENDER CHILD I SEE YOUR PINK NOSE

The moment comes (inexplicably)

Where I'm able to sit by your grave

And be audacious enough to entertain

The confusion swirling in my tiny brain

My paws till the earth

And plant seeds over you

Baby yellow roses

That will colorize this disconnected land

I promise

I'm not going to mourn anymore

But I won't stop grieving

For our innocent past

A past where responsibility didn't exist
And life was slightly more bearable
So strange to think of a time
Where I wasn't alone (I suppose I'm not)

I promise I'm going to nourish this land
To transform it
Grow it from these hardened roots
To a haven, extraordinarily lush

I cannot write poetry
Thus I am unable to force the world to remember you
But if my memory is enough
Then know your soul is immortalized

Thank you for the laughs
And sometimes the cries
And for those frustrating moments
Which taught me patience

A part of me is lost forever to the great beyond
I suppose there's nothing wrong with that
I know that when my time comes
That part will be waiting for me alongside you

I see your pink nose sticking out from the ground
And even though I cannot see your licorice face
I know you're probably laughing at me
For being such a crybaby

XIII

LASAGNA

EVERY DAY, EVERY NIGHT

The Earth has rotated once more

Pappa lets me lick his fingers

Girl chases me around the cat post

Boy is ecstatic I sleep on his chest again

Ma finds comfort in combing me

The moon has become less poetic

But no less pious

The air has become a bit more like water

Fluid and succulent

The land isn't barren anymore

The world isn't so terrifying anymore

Every day there is more love

Every night there are more dreams

The universe returns to equilibrium

ON THE SYNONYMOUS NATURE OF LIFE AND DEATH

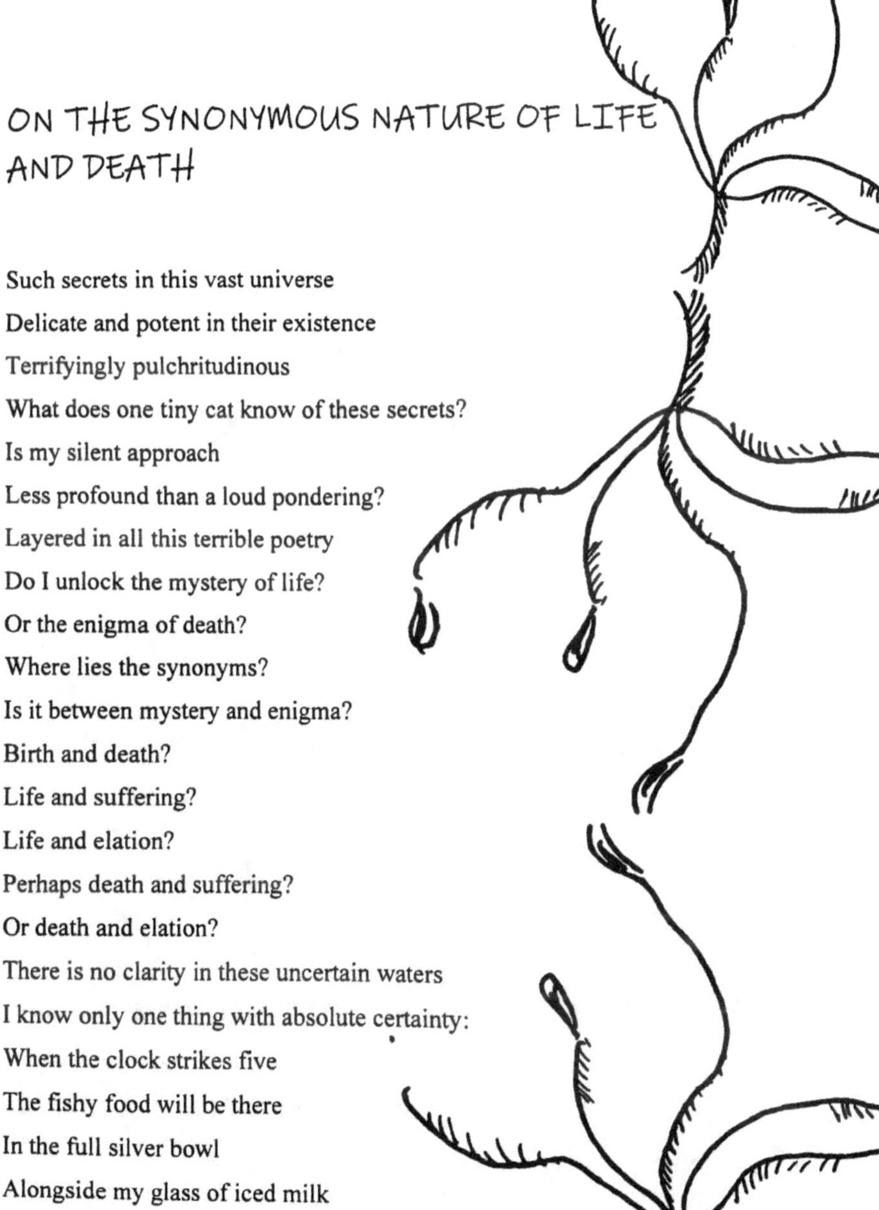

Such secrets in this vast universe

Delicate and potent in their existence

Terrifyingly pulchritudinous

What does one tiny cat know of these secrets?

Is my silent approach

Less profound than a loud pondering?

Layered in all this terrible poetry

Do I unlock the mystery of life?

Or the enigma of death?

Where lies the synonyms?

Is it between mystery and enigma?

Birth and death?

Life and suffering?

Life and elation?

Perhaps death and suffering?

Or death and elation?

There is no clarity in these uncertain waters

I know only one thing with absolute certainty:

When the clock strikes five

The fishy food will be there

In the full silver bowl

Alongside my glass of iced milk

Thank you for embarking on this uncertain journey with me.

www.ingramcontent.com/pod-product-compliance
Lightning Source LLC
Chambersburg PA
CBHW060911130726
48001CB00006B/2186